WEDDING READINGS
AND POEMS

WEDDING READINGS AND POEMS

Selection and preface by
BECKY BROWN

MACMILLAN COLLECTOR'S LIBRARY

This collection first published 2021 by Macmillan Collector's Library
an imprint of Pan Macmillan
The Smithson, 6 Briset Street, London EC1M 5NR
EU representative: Macmillan Publishers Ireland Limited, Mallard Lodge,
Lansdowne Village, Dublin 4
Associated companies throughout the world
www.panmacmillan.com

ISBN 978-1-5290-5259-6

Selection and preface © Becky Brown 2021
Additional material © COR Collective 2021

The permission acknowledgements on page 171–173
constitute an extension of this copyright page.

3 5 7 9 8 6 4

A CIP catalogue record for this book is available from the British Library.

Casing design and endpaper pattern by Andrew Davidson
Typeset in Plantin by Jouve (UK), Milton Keynes
Printed and bound in China by Imago

Visit **www.panmacmillan.com** to read more
about all our books and to buy them.

Contents

Preface xi

LOVE'S PHILOSOPHY

Love's Philosophy *Percy Bysshe Shelley* 3

from As You Like It *William Shakespeare* 4

'How do I love thee?' *Elizabeth Barrett Browning* 5

What Is Love *Sir Walter Raleigh* 6

Answer to a Child's Question
Samuel Taylor Coleridge 8

from Virginibus Puerisque *Robert Louis Stevenson* 9

First Love *John Clare* 10

Meeting at Night *Robert Browning* 12

My First Love Story *Rumi* 13

The Stolen Heart *Sir John Suckling* 14

To Elizabeth Barrett *Robert Browning* 16

A Ditty *Sir Philip Sidney* 17

All for Love *Lord Byron* 18

from The Great Gatsby *F. Scott Fitzgerald* 20

from A Backward Glance *Edith Wharton* 21

First Meeting *A. S. J. Tessimond* 22

The Call *Charlotte Mew* 24

Now *Robert Browning* 26

from Plato's Symposium *tr. Benjamin Jowett* 27

from The Hunting of Cupid *George Peele* 29

Renouncement *Alice Meynell* 30

THESE I CAN PROMISE

These I Can Promise *Mark Twain* 33

from The Book and the Brotherhood
Iris Murdoch 34

To a Friend *Amy Lowell* 35

Thee, Thee, Only Thee *Thomas Moore* 36

from Song of Solomon 38

To John Middleton Murry *Katherine Mansfield* 39

I Will Make You Brooches *Robert Louis Stevenson* 40

O Divine star of Heaven *John Fletcher* 41

Now You Will Feel No Rain *Apache wedding song* 42

The Bait *John Donne* 43

'i carry your heart with me (i carry it in my heart)'
E. E. Cummings 45

from Love Songs *Harriet Monroe* 47

from Song of the Open Road *Walt Whitman* 49

from Jane Eyre *Charlotte Brontë* 51

He Wishes for the Cloths of Heaven *W. B. Yeats* 52

Marriage Advice *Jane Wells* 53

Beauty That is Never Old *James Weldon Johnson* 54

Fragment *Letitia Elizabeth Landon* 55

from The Princess *Alfred, Lord Tennyson* 57

Have You Got a Biro I Can Borrow? *Clive James* 58

Since We Parted *Edward Robert Bulwer-Lytton* 60

Song—Come, let me take thee to my breast
Robert Burns 61

To My Excellent Lucasia, on Our Friendship
Katherine Philips 62

The Good-morrow *John Donne* 64

WHEN YOU ARE OLD

When You are Old *W. B. Yeats* 69

To Livy on her thirtieth birthday *Mark Twain* 70

Love and Friendship *Emily Brontë* 72

from Gift from the Sea *Anne Morrow Lindbergh* 73

'Bright Star! would I were steadfast as
thou art' *John Keats* 75

from Adam Bede *George Eliot* 76

An Hour with Thee *Sir Walter Scott* 77

Friendship *Henry David Thoreau* 79

Sonnet 18 *William Shakespeare* 82

from 'Monna Innominata: A Sonnet of Sonnets'
Christina Rossetti 83

When Two People Are At One 84

Marriage Morning *Alfred, Lord Tennyson* 85

from The Prophet *Kahlil Gibran* 87

If thou must love me, let it be for nought
Elizabeth Barrett Browning 88

Fidelity *D. H. Lawrence* 89

To My Dear and Loving Husband
Anne Bradstreet 92

from The Art of Marriage *Wilferd A. Peterson* 93

Love's Omnipresence *J. Sylvester* 95

from Endymion: A Poetic Romance *John Keats* 96

from Captain Corelli's Mandolin
Louis de Bernières 97

from 'The Hours of Afternoon' *Emile
Verhaeren tr. F. S. Flint* 98

Scaffolding *Seamus Heaney* 102

When We Are Old and These Rejoicing Veins *Edna
St. Vincent Millay* 103

from Great Expectations *Charles Dickens* 104

The True Beauty *T. Carew* 105

LOVE IS ENOUGH

from Love is Enough *William Morris* 109

A Birthday *Christina Rossetti* 110

To Fanny Brawne *John Keats* 111

from Colossians 113

We Two, How Long We Were Fool'd *Walt Whitman* 114

from Wuthering Heights *Emily Brontë* 116

If I Were Loved *Alfred, Lord Tennyson* 117

from Paradise Lost *John Milton* 118

Night Thoughts *Johann Wolfgang von Goethe* 119

Sonnet 116 *William Shakespeare* 120

First Sight of Her and After *Thomas Hardy* 121

When the Heart is Hard *Rabindranath Tagore* 122

from Portrait of a Lady *Henry James* 123

from Corinthians 124

from Discourse on the Passion of Love *Blaise Pascal tr. Orlando Williams Wight* 126

House of Dreams *Sara Teasdale* 128

Never Marry But For Love *William Penn* 129

A Moment *Mary Elizabeth Coleridge* 131

WEDDED BLISS

Wedded Bliss *Charlotte Perkins Gilman* 135

Love's Garden *Katharine Tynan* 137

from Les Misérables *Victor Hugo* 139

Wild Nights *Emily Dickinson* 140

O Solitude! if I must with thee dwell *John Keats* 141

from My Ántonia *Willa Cather* 142

from Song of Solomon 143

from To Althea, From Prison *Richard Lovelace* 144

Song *Christina Rossetti* 145

The Owl and the Pussy-Cat *Edward Lear* 146

from The Secret Garden *Frances Hodgson Burnett* 148

Friendship *Dinah Maria Craik* 150

Camomile Tea *Katherine Mansfield* 151

Love Song *Rainer Maria Rilke tr. Jessie Lamont* 152

from Emma *Jane Austen* 153

A Spring Morning *John Clare* 154

from 'The Bells' *Edgar Allan Poe* 155

from Chamber Music *James Joyce* 157

To-night *Sara Teasdale* 158

Public Speaking Tips 159

Index of Poets and Authors 161

Index of First Lines 165

Preface

There are few things more wonderful than standing together, just you and the person you love, in front of friends and family, and saying 'I do'. The journey to that moment is a long one; it doesn't matter whether you fell in love at first sight or started out as friends – building a committed relationship takes time and care. This is one of the reasons why planning a wedding is often such a lengthy process; devising a day that perfectly reflects who you are and why you are committing to each other will always naturally, and literally, be a labour of love.

Of all the decisions an engaged couple has to make, choosing which readings to use is often one of the most difficult. Whilst handwritten vows can be precisely tailored to the two of you, readings straddle a peculiar space between the personal and the ceremonial. A well-chosen extract or poem can encapsulate your feelings more powerfully than you could ever hope to manage with your own pen and paper. It's as if you are handing the job to an expert – just as you might order the cake from a baker or entrust the flowers to a professional florist – you can have the luxury of employing one of the great poets, novelists or philosophers to speak on your behalf.

The pieces here are selected with that desire for perfect expression held closely in mind, and all are suitable for reading aloud. From John Keats and Rabindranath Tagore, to Jane Austen, Iris Murdoch and Emily Dickinson, they are drawn from the loftiest heights of literature and from the works of many centuries, cultures and creeds. Together, they traverse every stage of courtship and commitment.

First is *Love's Philosophy*, which is brimming with the heady feeling of tumbling into love, then to *These I Can Promise*, full of the forging of bonds and making of vows. Next comes *When You Are Old*, made up of hope and intent for growing together and for all the pleasures a life-long relationship brings, then *Love is Enough*, which celebrates the sustaining and energizing abilities of love, and its extraordinary power to change and improve us. And finally, *Wedded Bliss*, for joy, fun, happiness and feelings that simply defy categorization. That these words written hundreds, if not thousands, of years ago can still beautifully epitomize a very modern, twenty-first-century love is a remarkable testament to the timeless and universal nature of love.

You will just *know* when you alight on the 'right' reading and, after the wedding, it will take on a new lifelong importance, occupying a special place in your heart and mind. So make sure to explore slowly, choose carefully and, most importantly, enjoy it. In the words of the writer and poet Katherine Mansfield, in a 1917 love letter to her future husband: 'We two, you know have everything before us, and we shall do very great things – I have perfect faith in us'.

LOVE'S PHILOSOPHY

Love's Philosophy

The fountains mingle with the river
And the rivers with the ocean.
The winds of heaven mix for ever
With a sweet emotion;
Nothing in the world is single,
All things by a law divine
In one another's being mingle –
Why not I with thine?

See the mountains kiss high heaven
And the waves clasp one another;
No sister-flower would be forgiven
If it disdain'd its brother:

And the sunlight clasps the earth,
And the moonbeams kiss the sea –
What are all these kissings worth,
If thou kiss not me?

Percy Bysshe Shelley (1792–1822)

from As You Like It
(Act V, Scene II)

No sooner met, but they look'd; no sooner
look'd, but they loved; no sooner loved, but they
sigh'd; no sooner sigh'd, but they ask'd one
another the reason; no sooner knew the reason,
but they sought the remedy: and in these degrees
have they made a pair of stairs to marriage.

William Shakespeare (1564–1616)

'How do I love thee?'
(Sonnets from the Portuguese, XLIII)

How do I love thee? Let me count the ways.
I love thee to the depth and breadth and
  height
My soul can reach, when feeling out of sight
For the ends of Being and ideal Grace.
I love thee to the level of everyday's
Most quiet need, by sun and candle-light.
I love thee freely, as men strive for Right:
I love thee purely, as they turn from Praise.
I love thee with the passion put to use
In my old griefs, and with my childhood's
  faith.
I love thee with a love I seemed to lose
With my lost saints! – I love thee with the
  breath,
Smiles, tears, of all my life! – and, if God
  choose,
I shall but love thee better after death.

Elizabeth Barrett Browning (1806–1861)

What Is Love

Now what is love, I pray thee tell?
It is that fountain and that well
Where pleasure and repentance dwell.
It is perhaps that saucing bell
That tolls all into heaven or hell:
And this is love, as I hear tell.

Yet what is love, I pray thee say?
It is a work on holy day.
It is December matched with May,
When lusty bloods in fresh array
Hear ten months after of the play:
And this is love, as I hear say.

Yet what is love, I pray thee sain?
It is a sunshine mixed with rain.
It is a toothache, or like pain;
It is a game where none doth gain;
The lass saith No, and would full fain:
And this is love, as I hear sain.

Yet what is love, I pray thee show?
A thing that creeps, it cannot go;

A prize that passeth to and fro;
A thing for one, a thing for mo;
And he that proves must find it so
And this is love, sweet friend, I trow.

Sir Walter Raleigh (c.1554–1618)

Answer to a Child's Question

Do you ask what the birds say? The Sparrow,
  the Dove,
The Linnet and Thrush say, 'I love and I
  love!'
In the winter they're silent – the wind is so
  strong;
What it says, I don't know, but it sings a loud
  song.
But green leaves, and blossoms, and sunny
  warm weather,
And singing, and loving – all come back
  together.
But the lark is so brimful of gladness and love,
The green fields below him, the blue sky
  above,
That he sings, and he sings; and for ever sings he –
'I love my Love, and my Love loves me!'

Samuel Taylor Coleridge (1772–1834)

from Virginibus Puerisque

Love should run out to meet love with open arms. Indeed, the ideal story is that of two people who go into love step for step, with a fluttered consciousness, like a pair of children venturing together into a dark room. From the first moment when they see each other, with a pang of curiosity, through stage after stage of growing pleasure and embarrassment, they can read the expression of their own trouble in each other's eyes. There is here no declaration properly so called; the feeling is so plainly shared, that as soon as the man knows what it is in his own heart, he is sure of what it is in the woman's.

Robert Louis Stevenson (1850–1894)

First Love

I ne'er was struck before that hour
  With love so sudden and so sweet
Her face it bloomed like a sweet flower
  And stole my heart away complete
My face turned pale a deadly pale
  My legs refused to walk away
And when she looked what could I ail
  My life and all seemed turned to clay

And then my blood rushed to my face
  And took my eyesight quite away
The trees and bushes round the place
  Seemed midnight at noon day
I could not see a single thing
  Words from my eyes did start
They spoke as chords do from the string
  And blood burnt round my heart

Are flowers the winter's choice
  Is love's bed always snow
She seemed to hear my silent voice
  Not love's appeals to know

I never saw so sweet a face
    As that I stood before
My heart has left its dwelling place
    And can return no more –

John Clare (1793–1864)

Meeting at Night

I

The grey sea and the long black land;
And the yellow half-moon large and low;
And the startled little waves that leap
In fiery ringlets from their sleep,
As I gain the cove with pushing prow,
And quench its speed i' the slushy sand.

II

Then a mile of warm sea-scented beach;
Three fields to cross till a farm appears;
A tap at the pane, the quick sharp scratch
And blue spurt of a lighted match,
And a voice less loud, through its joys and
    fears,
Than the two hearts beating each to each!

Robert Browning (1812–1889)

My First Love Story

The minute I heard my first love story
I started looking for you, not knowing
how blind that was.
Lovers don't finally meet somewhere.
They're in each other all along.

Rumi (1207–1273)

The Stolen Heart

I prithee send me back my heart,
Since I cannot have thine;
For if from yours you will not part,
Why then shouldst thou have mine?

Yet now I think on't, let it lie,
To find it were in vain;
For thou hast a thief in either eye
Would steal it back again.

Why should two hearts in one breast lie,
And yet not lodge together?
Love! where is thy sympathy,
If thus our breasts thou sever?

But love is such a mystery,
I cannot find it out;
For when I think I'm best resolved,
I then am in most doubt.

Then farewell care, and farewell woe;
I will no longer pine;

For I'll believe I have her heart,
As much as she hath mine.

Sir John Suckling (1609–1641)

To Elizabeth Barrett
On the morning of their wedding day,
12 September 1846

You will only expect a few words. What will those be? When the heart is full it may run over; but the real fullness stays within . . . Words can never tell you . . . how perfectly dear you are to me – perfectly dear to my heart and soul. I look back and in every one point, every word and gesture, every letter, every silence – you have been entirely perfect to me – I would not change one word, one look. My hope and aim are to preserve this love, not to fall from it – for which I trust to God, who procured it for me, and doubtless can preserve it. Enough now, my dearest own Ba! You have given me the highest, completest proof of love that ever one human being gave another. I am all gratitude – and all pride . . . that my life has been so crowned by you.

Robert Browning (1812–1889)

A Ditty

My true-love hath my heart, and I have his,
By just exchange one to the other given:
I hold his dear, and mine he cannot miss,
There never was a better bargain driven:
   My true-love hath my heart, and I have his.

His heart in me keeps him and me in one,
My heart in him his thoughts and senses
   guides:
He loves my heart, for once it was his own
I cherish his because in me it bides:
   My true-love hath my heart, and I have his.

Sir Philip Sidney (1554–1586)

All for Love

O talk not to me of a name great in story;
The days of our youth are the days of our
glory;
And the myrtle and ivy of sweet two-and-
twenty
Are worth all your laurels, though ever so
plenty.

What are garlands and crowns to the brow
that is wrinkled?
'Tis but as a dead flower with May-dew
besprinkled:
Then away with all such from the head that is
hoary—
What care I for the wreaths that can only give
glory?

O Fame!—if I e'er took delight in thy praises,
'Twas less for the sake of thy high-sounding
phrases,
Than to see the bright eyes of the dear one
discover

She thought that I was not unworthy to
   love her.

There chiefly I sought thee, there only I found
   thee;
Her glance was the best of the rays that
   surround thee;
When it sparkled o'er aught that was bright in
   my story,
I knew it was love, and I felt it was glory.

Lord Byron (1788–1824)

from The Great Gatsby

He smiled understandingly – much more than understandingly. It was one of those rare smiles with a quality of eternal reassurance in it, that you may come across four or five times in life. It faced – or seemed to face – the whole eternal world for an instant, and then concentrated on you with an irresistible prejudice in your favour.

It understood you just as far as you wanted to be understood, believed in you as you would like to believe in yourself, and assured you that it had precisely the impression of you that, at your best, you hoped to convey.

F. Scott Fitzgerald (1896–1940)

from A Backward Glance

I suppose there is one friend in the life of each of us who seems not a separate person, however dear and beloved, but an expansion, an interpretation, of one's self, the very meaning of one's soul.

Edith Wharton (1862–1937)

First Meeting
(to Diane)

When I first met you I knew I had come at
last home,
Home after wandering, home after long
puzzled searching,
Home after long being wind-borne, wave-
tossed, night-caught,
Long being lost;

And being with you as normal and needful
and natural
As sleeping or waking; and I was myself, who
had never
Been wholly myself; I was walking and talking
and laughing
Easily at last;

And the air was softer and sounds were
sharper
And colours were brighter and the sky was
higher
And length was not measured by milestones
and time was not measured by clocks . . .

And this end was a beginning . . .
And these words are the beginning of my
 thanks.

A. S. J. Tessimond (1902–1962)

The Call

From our low seat beside the fire
Where we have dozed and dreamed and
  watched the glow
Or raked the ashes, stopping so
We scarcely saw the sun or rain
Above, or looked much higher
Than this same quiet red or burned-out fire.
To-night we heard a call,
A rattle on the window-pane,
A voice on the sharp air,
And felt a breath stirring our hair,
A flame within us: Something swift and tall
Swept in and out and that was all.
Was it a bright or a dark angel? Who can
  know?
It left no mark upon the snow,
But suddenly it snapped the chain
Unbarred, flung wide the door
Which will not shut again;
And so we cannot sit here any more.

We must arise and go:
The world is cold without

And dark and hedged about
With mystery and enmity and doubt,
But we must go
Though yet we do not know
Who called, or what marks we shall leave
   upon the snow.

Charlotte Mew (1869–1928)

Now

Out of your whole life give but a moment!
All of your life that has gone before,
All to come after it, – so you ignore
So you make perfect the present, – condense,
In a rapture of rage, for perfection's
  endowment,
Thought and feeling and soul and sense –
Merged in a moment which gives me at last
You around me for once, you beneath me,
  above me –
Me – sure that despite of time future, time past, –
This tick of our life-time's one moment you
  love me!
How long such suspension may linger?
  Ah, Sweet –
The moment eternal – just that and no more –
When ecstasy's utmost we clutch at the core
While cheeks burn, arms open, eyes shut and
  lips meet!

Robert Browning (1812–1889)

from Plato's Symposium

And when one of them meets with his other half, the actual half of himself, whether he be a lover of youth or a lover of another sort, the pair are lost in an amazement of love and friendship and intimacy, and one will not be out of the other's sight, as I may say, even for a moment: these are the people who pass their whole lives together; yet they could not explain what they desire of one another. For the intense yearning which each of them has towards the other does not appear to be the desire of lover's intercourse, but of something else which the soul of either evidently desires and cannot tell, and of which she has only a dark and doubtful presentiment. Suppose Hephaestus, with his instruments, to come to the pair who are lying side by side and to say to them, 'What do you people want of one another?' they would be unable to explain. And suppose further, that when he saw their perplexity he said: 'Do you desire to be wholly one; always day and night to be in one another's company? for if this is what you desire, I am ready to melt you into one and let you grow together, so that being two you shall become one, and while you live a common life as if you were a single man, and after your death in the world below still be one departed soul instead of two – I ask whether this is what you lovingly desire, and whether you are satisfied to attain this?' – there is not a man of them who when he heard the proposal would deny or would not acknowledge that this meeting and melting into one another, this becoming one instead of two, was the very expression of his ancient need.

Plato, translated by Benjamin Jowett (1817–1893)

from The Hunting of Cupid

What thing is love? for, well I wot, love is a
   thing.
It is a prick, it is a sting,
It is a pretty pretty thing;
It is a fire, it is a coal,
Whose flame creeps in at every hole;
And as my wit doth best devise,
Love's dwelling is in ladies' eyes:
From whence do glance love's piercing darts
That make such holes into our hearts;
And all the world herein accord
Love is a great and mighty lord,
And when he list to mount so high,
With Venus he in heaven doth lie,
And evermore hath been a god
Since Mars and she played even and odd.

George Peele (1556–1596)

Renouncement

I must not think of thee; and, tired yet strong,
I shun the thought that lurks in all delight –
The thought of thee – and in the blue heaven's
    height,
And in the sweetest passage of a song.
O just beyond the fairest thoughts that throng
This breast, the thought of thee waits, hidden
    yet bright;
But it must never, never come in sight;
I must stop short of thee the whole day long.
But when sleep comes to close each difficult
    day,
When night gives pause to the long watch I
    keep,
And all my bonds I needs must loose apart,
And doff my will as raiment laid away, –
With the first dream that comes with the first
    sleep,
I run, I run, I am gathered to thy heart.

Alice Meynell (1847–1922)

THESE I CAN PROMISE

These I Can Promise

I cannot promise you a life of sunshine;
I cannot promise riches, wealth, or gold;
I cannot promise you an easy pathway
That leads away from change or growing old.

But I can promise all my heart's devotion
A smile to chase away your tears of sorrow;
A love that's ever true and ever growing;
A hand to hold in yours through each
    tomorrow.

Mark Twain (1835–1910)

from The Book and the Brotherhood

I hereby give myself. I love you. You are the only being whom I can love absolutely with my complete self, with all my flesh and mind and heart. You are my mate, my perfect partner, and I am yours. You must *feel* this now, as I do. It was a marvel that we ever met. It is some kind of divine luck that we are together now. We must never, never part again. We are, here, in this, *necessary* beings, like gods. As we look at each other we verify, we *know*, the perfection of our love, we *recognize* each other. *Here* is my life, here if need be is my death.

Iris Murdoch (1919–1999)

To a Friend

I ask but one thing of you, only one.
That you will always be my dream of you;
That never shall I wake to find untrue
All this I have believed and rested on,
Forever vanished, like a vision gone
Out into the night. Alas, how few
There are who strike in us a chord we knew
Existed, but so seldom heard its tone
We tremble at the half-forgotten sound.
The world is full of rude awakenings
And heaven-born castles shattered to the
    ground,
Yet still our human longing vainly clings
To a belief in beauty through all wrongs.
O stay your hand, and leave my heart its
    songs!

Amy Lowell (1874–1925)

Thee, Thee, Only Thee

The dawning of morn, the daylight's sinking.
The night's long hours still find me thinking
    Of thee, thee, only thee.
When friends are met, and goblets crown'd,
  And smiles are near that once enchanted,
Unreach'd by all that sunshine round,
   My soul, like some dark spot, is haunted
    By thee, thee, only thee.

Whatever in fame's high path could waken
My spirit once, is now forsaken
    For thee, thee, only thee.
Like shores, by which some headlong bark
  To the ocean hurries, resting never,
Life's scenes go by me, bright or dark
   I know not, heed not, hastening ever
    To thee, thee, only thee.

I have not a joy but of thy bringing,
And pain itself seems sweet when springing
    From thee, thee, only thee.
Like spells that naught on earth can break,
  Till lips that know the charm have spoken,

This heart, howe'er the world may wake
Its grief, its scorn, can but be broken
By thee, thee, only thee.

Thomas Moore (1779–1852)

from Song of Solomon

Chapter 8, Verses 6–7

Set me as a seal upon your heart,
  as a seal upon your arm;
for love is strong as death,
  passion fierce as the grave.
Its flashes are flashes of fire,
  a raging flame.
Many waters cannot quench love,
  neither can floods drown it.
If one offered for love
  all the wealth of one's house,
  it would be utterly scorned.

To John Middleton Murry
Sent from 24 Redcliffe Road, Fulham
Saturday night, 18 May 1917

My darling
Do not imagine, because you find these lines in
your private book that I have been trespassing.
You know I have not – and where else shall I
leave a love letter? For I long to write you a love
letter tonight. You are all about me – I seem to
breathe you – hear you – feel you in me and of
me – What am I doing here? You are away – I
have seen you in the train, at the station, driving
up, sitting in the lamplight talking, greeting
people – washing your hands – And I am here –
in your tent – sitting at your table. [. . .] We two,
you know have everything before us, and we
shall do very great things – I have perfect faith in
us – and so perfect is my love for you that I am,
as it were, still, silent to my very soul. I want
nobody but you for my lover and my friend and
to nobody but you shall I be *faithful*.

I am yours for ever.

Katherine Mansfield (1888–1923)

· 39 ·

I Will Make You Brooches

I will make you brooches and toys for your
   delight
Of bird-song at morning and star-shine at
   night.
I will make a palace fit for you and me,
Of green days in forests and blue days at sea.

I will make my kitchen, and you shall keep
   your room,
Where white flows the river and bright blows
   the broom,
And you shall wash your linen and keep your
   body white
In rainfall at morning and dewfall at night.

And this shall be for music when no one else
   is near,
The fine song for singing, the rare song to hear!
That only I remember, that only you admire,
Of the broad road that stretches and the
   roadside fire.

Robert Louis Stevenson (1850–1894)

O Divine star of Heaven

O divine star of Heaven,
Thou in power above the seven;
Thou sweet kindler of desires
Till they grow to mutual fires;
Thou, O gentle Queen, that art
Curer of each wounded heart;
Thou the fuel, and the flame;
Thou in heaven, and here, the same;
Thou the wooer, and the wooed;
Thou the hunger; and the food;
Thou the prayer and the prayed;
Thou what is or shall be said.
Thou still young, and golden tressed,
Make me by thy answer blessed.

John Fletcher (1579–1625)

Now You Will Feel No Rain

Apache wedding song

Now you will feel no rain,
for each of you will be a shelter to the other.

Now you will feel no cold,
for each of you will be warmth to the other.

Now there will be no loneliness,
for each of you will be a comfort to the other.

Now you are two persons,
but there is only one life before you.

Go now to your dwelling place,
to enter into the days of your togetherness.

And may your days be good
and long upon the earth.

The Bait

Come live with me, and be my love,
And we will some new pleasures prove
Of golden sands and crystal brooks,
With silken lines and silver hooks.

There will the river whispering run
Warmed by thy eyes, more than the sun.
And there the'enamoured fish will stay,
Begging themselves they may betray.

When thou wilt swim in that live bath,
Each fish, which every channel hath,
Will amorously to thee swim,
Gladder to catch thee, than thou him.

If thou, to be so seen, be'st loth,
By sun, or moon, thou darkenest both,
And if myself have leave to see,
I need not their light, having thee.

Let others freeze with angling reeds,
And cut their legs with shells and weeds,

Or treacherously poor fish beset,
With strangling snare or windowy net:

Let coarse bold hands, from slimy nest
The bedded fish in banks out-wrest,
Or curious traitors, sleavesilk flies
Bewitch poor fishes' wandering eyes.

For thee, thou need'st no such deceit,
For thou thyself art thine own bait:
That fish, that is not catched thereby,
Alas, is wiser far than I.

John Donne (1572–1631)

'i carry your heart with me
(i carry it in my heart)'

i carry your heart with me (i carry it in
my heart) i am never without it (anywhere
i go you go, my dear and whatever is done
by only me is your doing, my darling)
                                        i fear;
no fate (for you are my fate, my sweet) i want
no world (for beautiful you are my world, my
   true)
and it's you are whatever a moon has always
   meant
and whatever a sun will always sing is you

here is the deepest secret nobody knows
(here is the root of the root and the bud of the
   bud
and the sky of the sky of a tree called life;
   which grows
higher than soul can hope or mind can hide)
and this is the wonder that's keeping the stars
   apart

i carry your heart (i carry it in my heart)

E. E. Cummings (1894–1962)

from Love Songs

I

I love my life, but not too well
  To give it to thee like a flower,
So it may pleasure thee to dwell
  Deep in its perfume but an hour.
I love my life, but not too well.

I love my life, but not too well
  To sing it note by note away,
So to thy soul the song may tell
  The beauty of the desolate day.
I love my life, but not too well.

I love my life, but not too well
  To cast it like a cloak on thine,
Against the storms that sound and swell
  Between thy lonely heart and mine.
I love my life, but not too well.

II

Your love is like a blue blue wave
  The little rainbows play in.
Your love is like a mountain cave
  Cool shadows darkly stay in.

It thrills me like great gales at war,
  It soothes like softest singing.
It bears me where clear rivers are,
  With reeds and rushes swinging;
Or out to pearly shores afar
  Where temple bells are ringing.

Harriet Monroe (1860–1936)

from Song of the Open Road

Listen! I will be honest with you,
I do not offer the old smooth prizes, but offer
   rough new prizes,
These are the days that must happen to you:
You shall not heap up what is called riches,
You shall scatter with lavish hand all that you
   earn or achieve . . .

Allons! After the great Companions, and to
   belong to them!
They too are on the road – they are the swift
   and majestic men –
              they are the greatest women,
Enjoyers of calm seas and storms of seas,
Sailors of many a ship, walkers of many a mile
   of land,
Habitués of many distant countries, habitués
   of far-distant dwellings,
Trusters of men and women, observers of
   cities, solitary toilers,
Pausers and contemplators of tufts, blossoms,
   shells of the shore,

Dancers at wedding-dances, kissers of brides,
  tender helpers of children,
               bearers of children . . .

Camerado, I give you my hand!
I give you my love more precious than money,
I give you myself before preaching or law;
Will you give me yourself? will you come
  travel with me?
Shall we stick by each other as long as we live?

Walt Whitman (1819–1892)

from Jane Eyre

I have for the first time found what I can truly love – I have found *you*. You are my sympathy – my better self – my good angel. I am bound to you with a strong attachment. I think you good, gifted, lovely: a fervent, a solemn passion is conceived in my heart; it leans to you, draws you to my centre and spring of life, wraps my existence about you, and, kindling in pure, powerful flame, fuses you and me in one.

Charlotte Brontë (1816–1855)

He Wishes for the Cloths of Heaven

Had I the heavens' embroidered cloths,
Enwrought with golden and silver light,
The blue and the dim and the dark cloths
Of night and light and the half-light,
I would spread the cloths under your feet:
But I, being poor, have only my dreams;
I have spread my dreams under your feet;
Tread softly because you tread on my dreams.

W. B. Yeats (1865–1939)

Marriage Advice

Let your love be stronger than your hate or
   anger.
Learn the wisdom of compromise, for it is
   better to bend a little than to break.
Believe the best rather than the worst.
People have a way of living up or down to your
   opinion of them.
Remember that true friendship is the basis for
   any lasting relationship. The person you
   choose to marry is deserving of the courtesies
   and kindness you bestow on your friends.
Please hand this down to your children and
   your children's children. The more things
   change the more they are the same.

Jane Wells (1807–1856)

Beauty That is Never Old

When buffeted and beaten by life's storms,
When by the bitter cares of life oppressed,
I want no surer haven than your arms,
I want no sweeter heaven than your breast.

When over my life's way there falls the blight
Of sunless days, and nights of starless skies;
Enough for me, the calm and steadfast light
That softly shines within your loving eyes.

The world, for me, and all the world can hold
Is circled by your arms; for me there lies,
Within the lights and shadows of your eyes,
The only beauty that is never old.

James Weldon Johnson (1871–1938)

Fragment

Love thee! yes, yes! the storms that rend aside
All other ties will but entwine my heart
More closely, more devotedly to thine.
Love thee!—but that I know how heavily
Sorrow hath press'd thy generous spirit down,
I should almost reproach thee for the doubt!
I have no thought, that does not dwell on thee;
No hope, in which thou minglest not; no wish,
In which thou bearest no part; my orisons
To heaven, begin and end with thy dear name:
My fate is link'd with thine—I did not plight
My vows to thee for a mere summer day,
But still to be unchang'd; it was most sweet
To share thy sunlight of prosperity,
Thine hours of brightness; now I only ask
To share thy sorrow, and to be to thee
All tenderness, and love, and constancy—
A feeling, lighting up thy desolate heart;
A fountain springing in the wilderness;

Or as the breeze upon the fever'd brow,
Soothing the pain it may not chase away.

Letitia Elizabeth Landon (1802–1838)

from The Princess

Now sleeps the crimson petal, now the white;
Nor waves the cypress in the palace walk;
Nor winks the gold fin in the porphyry font.
The firefly wakens; waken thou with me.

   Now droops the milk-white peacock like a
     ghost,
And like a ghost she glimmers on to me.

   Now lies the Earth all Danaë to the stars,
And all thy heart lies open unto me.

   Now slides the silent meteor on, and leaves
A shining furrow, as thy thoughts in me.

   Now folds the lily all her sweetness up,
And slips into the bosom of the lake.
So fold thyself, my dearest, thou, and slip
Into my bosom and be lost in me.

Alfred, Lord Tennyson (1809–1892)

Have You Got a Biro I Can Borrow?

Have you got a biro I can borrow?
I'd like to write your name
On the palm of my hand, on the walls of the
  hall
The roof of the house, right across the land
So when the sun comes up tomorrow
It'll look to this side of the hard-bitten planet
Like a big yellow button with your name
  written on it

Have you got a biro I can borrow?
I'd like to write some lines
In praise of your knee, and the back of your
  neck
And the double-decker bus that brings you
  to me
So when the sun comes up tomorrow
It'll shine on a world made richer by a sonnet
And a half-dozen epics as long as the *Aeneid*

Oh give me a pen and some paper
Give me a chisel or a camera
A piano and a box of rubber bands

I need room for choreography
And a darkroom for photography
Tie the brush into my hands

Have you got a biro I can borrow?
I'd like to write your name
From the belt of Orion to the share of the
   Plough
The snout of the Bear to the belly of the Lion
So when the sun goes down tomorrow
There'll never be a minute
Not a moment of the night that hasn't got you
   in it

Clive James (1939–2019)

Since We Parted

Since we parted yester eve,
I do love thee, love, believe,
Twelve times dearer, twelve hours longer,—
One dream deeper, one night stronger,
One sun surer,—thus much more
Than I loved thee, love, before.

Edward Robert Bulwer-Lytton (1831–1891)

Song—Come, let me take thee to my breast

Come, let me take thee to my breast,
  And pledge we ne'er shall sunder;
And I shall spurn as vilest dust
  The world's wealth and grandeur:
And do I hear my Jeanie own
  That equal transports move her?
I ask for dearest life alone,
  That I may live to love her.

Thus, in my arms, wi' a' her charms,
  I clasp my countless treasure;
I'll seek nae main o' Heav'n to share,
  Tha sic a moment's pleasure:
And by thy e'en sae bonie blue,
  I swear I'm thine for ever!
And on thy lips I seal my vow,
  And break it shall I never.

Robert Burns (1759–1796)

To My Excellent Lucasia,
on Our Friendship

I did not live until this time
  Crowned my felicity,
When I could say without a crime,
  I am not thine, but thee.

This carcass breathed, and walked, and slept,
  So that the world believed
There was a soul the motions kept;
  But they were all deceived.

For as a watch by art is wound
  To motion, such was mine:
But never had Orinda found
  A soul till she found thine;

Which now inspires, cures and supplies,
  And guides my darkened breast:
For thou art all that I can prize,
  My joy, my life, my rest.

No bridegroom's nor crown-conqueror's mirth
  To mine compared can be:

They have but pieces of the earth,
   I've all the world in thee.

Then let our flames still light and shine,
   And no false fear control,
As innocent as our design,
   Immortal as our soul.

Katherine Philips (1632–1664)

The Good-morrow

I wonder by my troth, what thou and I
Did, till we loved? were we not weaned till
  then?
But sucked on country pleasures, childishly?
Or snorted we in the seven sleepers' den?
'Twas so; but this, all pleasures fancies be.
If ever any beauty I did see,
Which I desired, and got, 'twas but a dream of
  thee.

And now good-morrow to our waking souls,
Which watch not one another out of fear;
For love all love of other sights controls,
And makes one little room an everywhere.
Let sea-discoverers to new worlds have gone,
Let maps to other, worlds on worlds have
  shown,
Let us possess one world, each hath one, and
  is one.

My face in thine eye, thine in mine appears,
And true plain hearts do in the faces rest;
Where can we find two better hemispheres

Without sharp North, without declining West?
What ever dies, was not mixed equally;
If our two loves be one, or thou and I
Love so alike that none do slacken, none
   can die.

John Donne (1573–1631)

WHEN YOU ARE OLD

When You are Old

When you are old and grey and full of sleep,
And nodding by the fire, take down this book,
And slowly read, and dream of the soft look
Your eyes had once, and of their shadows
   deep;

How many loved your moments of glad grace,
And loved your beauty with love false or true,
But one man loved the pilgrim soul in you,
And loved the sorrows of your changing face;

And bending down beside the glowing bars,
Murmur, a little sadly, how Love fled
And paced upon the mountains overhead
And hid his face amid a crowd of stars.

W. B. Yeats (1865–1939)

To Livy on her thirtieth birthday
Hartford, 27 November 1875

Livy darling,

Six years have gone by since I made my first great success in life and won you, and thirty years have passed since Providence made preparation for that happy success by sending you into the world. Every day we live together adds to the security of my confidence, that we can never any more wish to be separated than that we can ever imagine a regret that we were ever joined. You are dearer to me to-day, my child, than you were upon the last anniversary of this birth-day; you were dearer then than you were a year before – you have grown more and more dear from the first of those anniversaries, and I do not doubt that this precious progression will continue on to the end.

Let us look forward to the coming anniversaries, with their age and their gray hairs without fear and without depression, trusting and believing that the love we bear each other will be sufficient to make them blessed.

So, with abounding affection for you and our

babies, I hail this day that brings you the matronly grace and dignity of three decades!

Always Yours

S. L. C.

Mark Twain (1835–1910)

Love and Friendship

Love is like the wild rose briar,
Friendship, like the holly tree
The holly is dark when the rose briar blooms,
But which will bloom most constantly?

The wild rose briar is sweet in spring,
Its summer blossoms scent the air
Yet wait till winter comes again
And who will call the wild-briar fair?

Then scorn the silly rose-wreath now
And deck thee with the holly's sheen
That when December blights thy brow
He still may leave thy garland green –

Emily Brontë (1818–1848)

from Gift from the Sea

When you love someone you do not love them all the time, in exactly the same way, from moment to moment. It is an impossibility. It is even a lie to pretend to. And yet this is exactly what most of us demand. We have so little faith in the ebb and flow of life, of love, of relationships. We leap at the flow of the tide and resist in terror its ebb. We are afraid it will never return. We insist on permanency, on duration, on continuity; when the only continuity possible, in life as in love, is in growth, in fluidity – in freedom, in the sense that the dancers are free, barely touching as they pass, but partners in the same pattern. The only real security is not in owning or possessing, not in demanding or expecting, not in hoping, even. Security in a relationship lies neither in looking back to what it was in nostalgia, nor forward to what it might be in dread or anticipation, but living in the present relationship and accepting it as it is now. For relationships, too, must be like islands. One must accept them for what they are here and now, within their limits – islands, surrounded and interrupted by the sea, continually visited and abandoned by the tides.

Anne Morrow Lindbergh (1906–2001)

'Bright Star! would I were steadfast as thou art'

Bright Star! would I were steadfast as thou art –
Not in lone splendour hung aloft the night,
And watching, with eternal lids apart,
Like Nature's patient sleepless Eremite,
The moving waters at their priestlike task
Of pure ablution round earth's human shores,
Or gazing on the new soft-fallen mask
Of snow upon the mountains and the moors –
No – yet still steadfast, still unchangeable,
Pillowed upon my fair love's ripening breast
To feel for ever its soft fall and swell,
Awake for ever in a sweet unrest;
Still, still to hear her tender-taken breath,
And so live ever – or else swoon to death.

John Keats (1795–1821)

from Adam Bede

What greater thing is there for two human souls than to feel that they are joined together for life—to strengthen each other in all labour, to rest on each other in all sorrow, to minister to each other in all pain, to be one with each other in the silent unspeakable memories at the moment of the last parting?

George Eliot (1819–1880)

An Hour with Thee

An hour with thee! When earliest day
Dapples with gold the eastern grey,
Oh, what can frame my mind to bear
The toil and turmoil, cark and care,
New griefs, which coming hours unfold,
And sad remembrance of the old?
    One hour with thee.

One hour with thee! When burning June
Waves his red flag at pitch of noon;
What shall repay the faithful swain,
His labour on the sultry plain;
And, more than cave or sheltering bough,
Cool feverish blood and throbbing brow?
    One hour with thee.

One hour with thee! When sun is set,
Oh, what can teach me to forget
The thankless labours of the day;
The hopes, the wishes, flung away;
The increasing wants, and lessening gains,

The master's pride, who scorns my pains?
  One hour with thee.

Sir Walter Scott (1771–1832)

Friendship

I think awhile of Love, and while I think,
    Love is to me a world,
    Sole meat and sweetest drink,
    And close connecting link
      'Tween heaven and earth.

I only know it is, not how or why,
    My greatest happiness;
    However hard I try,
    Not if I were to die,
      Can I explain.

I fain would ask my friend how it can be,
    But when the time arrives,
    Then Love is more lovely
    Than anything to me,
      And so I'm dumb.

For if the truth were known, Love cannot
  speak,
    But only thinks and does;
    Though surely out 't will leak

Without the help of Greek,
    Or any tongue.

A man may love the truth and practise it,
    Beauty he may admire,
    And goodness not omit,
    As much as may befit
      To reverence.

But only when these three together meet,
    As they always incline,
    And make one soul the seat,
    And favourite retreat,
      Of loveliness;

When under kindred shape, like loves and
  hates
    And a kindred nature,
    Proclaim us to be mates,
    Exposed to equal fates
      Eternally;

And each may other help, and service do,
    Drawing Love's bands more tight,
    Service he ne'er shall rue

While one and one make two,
  And two are one;

In such case only doth man fully prove
    Fully as man can do,
    What power there is in Love
    His inmost soul to move
      Resistlessly.

Two sturdy oaks I mean, which side by side,
    Withstand the winter's storm,
    And spite of wind and tide,
    Grow up the meadow's pride,
      For both are strong.

Above they barely touch, but undermined
    Down to their deepest source,
    Admiring you shall find
    Their roots are intertwined
      Insep'rably

Henry David Thoreau (1817–1862)

Sonnet 18

Shall I compare thee to a summer's day?
Thou art more lovely and more temperate:
Rough winds do shake the darling buds of May,
And summer's lease hath all too short a date:
Sometime too hot the eye of heaven shines,
And often is his gold complexion dimm'd,
And every fair from fair sometime declines,
By chance or natures changing course
  untrimm'd:
But thy eternal summer shall not fade,
Nor lose possession of that fair thou owest,
Nor shall death brag thou wandrest in his
  shade,
When in eternal lines to time thou growest,
    So long as men can breathe or eyes
      can see
    So long lives this, and this gives life to
      thee.

William Shakespeare (1564–1616)

from 'Monna Innominata:
A Sonnet of Sonnets'

IV

I loved you first: but afterwards your love
Outsoaring mine, sang such a loftier song
As drowned the friendly cooings of my dove.
Which owes the other most? My love was long,
And yours one moment seemed to wax more
    strong;
I loved and guessed at you, you construed me
And loved me for what might or might not be –
Nay, weights and measures do us both a wrong.
For verily love knows not 'mine' or 'thine';
With separate 'I' and 'thou' free love has done,
For one is both and both are one in love:
Rich love knows naught of 'thine that is not
    mine';
Both have the strength and both the length
    thereof,
Both of us, of the love which makes us one.

Christina Rossetti (1830–1894)

When Two People Are At One
(*from* I Ching)

When two people are at one in their inmost
  hearts,
They shatter even the strength of iron or of
  bronze.
And when two people understand each other
  in their inmost hearts,
Their words are sweet and strong, like the
  fragrance of orchids.

Marriage Morning

Light, so low upon earth,
   You send a flash to the sun.
Here is the golden dose of love,
   All my wooing is done.
Oh, the woods and the meadows,
   Woods where we hid from the wet,
Stiles where we stayed to be kind,
   Meadows in which we met!

Light, so low in the vale
   You flash and lighten afar;
For this is the golden morning of love,
   And you are his morning star.
Flash, I am coming, I come,
   By meadow and stile and wood,
Oh, lighten into my eyes and heart,
   Into my heart and my blood!

Heart, are you great enough
   For a love that never tires?
O heart, are you great enough for love?
   I have heard of thorns and briers.
Over the thorns and briers,

Over the meadow and stiles,
Over the world to the end of it
Flash for a million miles.

Alfred, Lord Tennyson (1809–1892)

from The Prophet

Love has no other desire but to fulfil itself.
But if you love and must needs have desires,
   let these be your desires:
To melt and be like a running brook that sings
   its melody to the night.
To know the pain of too much tenderness.
To be wounded by your own understanding of
   love;
And to bleed willingly and joyfully.
To wake at dawn with a winged heart and give
   thanks for another day of loving;
To rest at the noon hour and meditate love's
   ecstasy;
To return home at eventide with gratitude;
And then to sleep with a prayer for the beloved
   in your heart and a song of praise on your lips.

Kahlil Gibran (1883–1931)

If thou must love me, let it be for nought
(Sonnets from the Portuguese, XIV)

If thou must love me, let it be for nought
Except for love's sake only. Do not say
'I love her for her smile . . . her look . . . her way
Of speaking gently, . . . for a trick of thought
That falls in well with mine, and certes brought
A sense of pleasant ease on such a day' –
For these things in themselves, Beloved, may
Be changed, or change for thee, – and love, so
   wrought,
May be unwrought so. Neither love me for
Thine own dear pity's wiping my cheeks dry,
Since one might well forget to weep who bore
Thy comfort long, and lose thy love thereby.
But love me for love's sake, that evermore
Thou may'st love on through love's eternity,

Elizabeth Barrett Browning (1806–1861)

Fidelity

Fidelity and love are two different things, like
  a flower and a gem.
And love, like a flower, will fade, will change
  into something else
or it would not be flowery.

O flowers they fade because they are moving
  swiftly; a little torrent of life
leaps up to the summit of the stem, gleams,
  turns over round the bend
of the parabola of curved flight,
sinks, and is gone, like a cornet curving into
  the invisible.

O flowers they are all the time travelling
like cornets, and they come into our ken
for a day, for two days, and withdraw, slowly
  vanish again.

And we, we must take them on the wing, and
  let them go.
Embalmed flowers are not flowers, immortelles
  are not flowers;

flowers are just a motion, a swift motion, a
    coloured gesture;
that is their loveliness. And that is love.

But a gem is different. It lasts so much longer
    than we do
so much much much longer
that it seems to last forever.
Yet we know it is flowing away
as flowers are, and we are, only slower.
The wonderful slow flowing of the sapphire!

All flows, and every flow is related to every
    other flow.
Flowers and sapphires and us, diversely
    streaming.
In the old days, when sapphires were breathed
    upon and brought forth
during the wild orgasms of chaos
time was much slower, when the rocks came
    forth.
It took aeons to make a sapphire, aeons for it
    to pass away.

And a flower it takes a summer.

And man and woman are like the earth, that
   brings forth flowers
in summer, and love, but underneath is rock.
Older than flowers, older than ferns, older
   than foraminiferae
older than plasm altogether is the soul of a
   man underneath.

And when, throughout all the wild orgasms of
   love
slowly a gem forms, in the ancient, once-
   more-molten rocks
of two human hearts, two ancient rocks, a
   man's heart and a woman's,
that is the crystal of peace, the slow hard jewel
   of trust,
the sapphire of fidelity.
The gem of mutual peace emerging from the
   wild chaos of love.

D. H. Lawrence (1885–1930)

To My Dear and Loving Husband

If ever two were one, then surely we.
If ever man were loved by wife, then thee;
If ever wife was happy in a man,
Compare with me ye women if you can
I prize thy love more than whole mines of gold,
Or all the riches that the East doth hold.
My love is such that rivers cannot quench,
Nor ought but love from thee give recompense.
Thy love is such I can no way repay;
The heavens reward thee manifold, I pray,
Then while we live, in love let's so persever,
That when we live no more we may live ever.

Anne Bradstreet (1612–1672)

from The Art of Marriage

A good marriage must be created.

In the marriage, the little things are the big things.

It is never being too old to hold hands.

It is remembering to say 'I love you' at least once each day.

It is never going to sleep angry.

It is having a mutual sense of values and objectives.

It is standing together and facing the world.

It is forming a circle of love that gathers in the whole family.

It is speaking words of appreciation and demonstrating gratitude in thoughtful ways.

It is having the capacity to forgive and forget.

It is giving each other an atmosphere in which each person can grow.

It is a common search for the good and the beautiful.

It is not only marrying the right person; it is being the right partner.

Wilferd A. Peterson (1900–1995)

Love's Omnipresence

Were I as base as is the lowly plain,
And you, my Love, as high as heaven above,
Yet should the thoughts of me your humble
  swain
Ascend to heaven, in honour of my Love.

Were I as high as heaven above the plain,
And you, my Love, as humble and as low
As are the deepest bottoms of the main,
Whereso'er you were, with you my love
  should go.

Were you the earth, dear Love, and I the skies,
My love should shine on you like to the sun,
And look upon you with ten thousand eyes
Till heaven wax'd blind, and till the world
  were done.

Whereso'er I am, below, or else above you,
Whereso'er you are, my heart shall truly
  love you.

J. Sylvester (1563–1618)

from Endymion: A Poetic Romance

A thing of beauty is a joy for ever:
Its loveliness increases; it will never
Pass into nothingness; but still will keep
A bower quiet for us, and a sleep
Full of sweet dreams, and health, and quiet
   breathing.

John Keats (1795–1821)

from Captain Corelli's Mandolin

Love is a temporary madness, it erupts like volcanoes and then subsides. And when it subsides you have to make a decision. You have to work out whether your root was so entwined together that it is inconceivable that you should ever part. Because this is what love is.

Love is not breathlessness, it is not excitement, it is not the promulgation of promises of eternal passion. That is just being 'in love', which any fool can do. Love itself is what is left over when being in love has burned away, and this is both an art and a fortunate accident.

Those that truly love have roots that grow towards each other underground, and when all the pretty blossoms have fallen from their branches, they find that they are one tree and not two.

Louis de Bernières (1945–)

from 'The Hours of Afternoon'

I

Step by step, day by day, age has come and placed his hands upon the bare forehead of our love, and has looked upon it with his dimmer eyes.

And in the fair garden shrivelled by July, the flowers, the groves and the living leaves have let fall something of their fervid strength on to the pale pond and the gentle paths. Here and there, the sun, harsh and envious, marks a hard shadow around his light.

And yet the hollyhocks still persist in their growth towards their final splendour, and the seasons weigh upon our life in vain; more than ever, all the roots of our two hearts plunge unsatiated into happiness, and clutch, and sink deeper.

Oh! these hours of afternoon girt with roses that twine around time, and rest against his benumbed flanks with cheeks aflower and aflame!

And nothing, nothing is better than to feel thus, still happy and serene, after how many years? But if our destiny had been quite different, and we had both been called upon to suffer—even then!—oh! I should have been happy to live and die, without complaining, in my stubborn love.

II

Roses of June, you the fairest with your hearts transfixed by the sun; violent and tranquil roses, like a delicate flock of birds settled on the branches;

Roses of June and July, upright and new, mouths and kisses that suddenly move or grow still with the coming and going of the wind, caress of shadow and gold on the restless garden;

Roses of mute ardour and gentle will, roses of voluptuousness in your mossy sheaths, you who spend the days of high summer loving each other in the brightness;

Fresh, glowing, magnificent roses, all our roses, oh! that, like you, our manifold desires, in our dear weariness or trembling pleasure, might love and exalt each other and rest!

III

If other flowers adorn the house and the splendour of the countryside, the pure ponds shine still in the grass with the great eyes of water of their mobile face.

Who can say from what far-off and unknown distances so many new birds have come with sun on their wings?

In the garden, April has given way to July, and the blue tints to the great carnation tints; space is warm and the wind frail; a thousand insects glisten joyously in the air; and summer passes in her robe of diamonds and sparks.

IV

The darkness is lustral and the dawn iridescent. From the lofty branch whence a bird flies, the dew-drops fall.

A lucid and frail purity adorns a morning so bright that prisms seem to gleam in the air. A spring babbles; a noise of wings is heard.

Oh! how beautiful are your eyes at that first hour when our silver ponds shimmer in the light and reflect the day that is rising. Your forehead is radiant and your blood beats.

Intense and wholesome life in all its divine strength enters your bosom so completely, like a driving happiness, that to contain its anguish and its fury, your hands suddenly take mine, and press them almost fearfully against your heart.

Emile Verhaeren, translated by F. S. Flint
(1855–1906 and 1885–1960)

Scaffolding

Masons, when they start upon a building,
Are careful to test out the scaffolding;

Make sure that planks won't slip at busy
   points,
Secure all ladders, tighten bolted joints.

And yet all this comes down when the job's
   done
Showing off walls of sure and solid stone.

So if, my dear, there sometimes seem to be
Old bridges breaking between you and me

Never fear. We can let the scaffolds fall
Confident that we have built our wall.

Seamus Heaney (1939–2013)

When We Are Old and
These Rejoicing Veins

When we are old and these rejoicing veins
Are frosty channels to a muted stream,
And out of all our burning their remains
No feeblest spark to fire us, even in dream,
This be our solace: that it was not said
When we were young and warm and in our
   prime,
Upon our couch we lay as lie the dead,
Sleeping away the unreturning time.
O sweet, O heavy-lidded, O my love,
When morning strikes her spear upon the
   land,
And we must rise and arm us and reprove
The insolent daylight with a steady hand,
Be not discountenanced if the knowing know
We rose from rapture but an hour ago.

Edna St. Vincent Millay (1892–1950)

from Great Expectations

You are part of my existence, part of myself. You have been in every line I have ever read, since I first came here [. . .] You have been in every prospect I have ever seen since – on the river, on the sails of the ships, on the marshes, in the clouds, in the light, in the darkness, in the wind, in the woods, in the sea, in the streets. You have been the embodiment of every graceful fancy that my mind has ever become acquainted with. The stones of which the strongest London buildings are made, are not more real, or more impossible to be displaced by your hands, than your presence and influence have been to me, there and everywhere, and will be.

Charles Dickens (1912–1870)

The True Beauty

He that loves a rosy cheek
   Or a coral lip admires,
Or from star-like eyes doth seek
   Fuel to maintain his fires;
As old Time makes these decay,
So his flames must waste away.

But a smooth and steadfast mind,
   Gentle thoughts, and calm desires,
Hearts with equal love combined,
   Kindle never-dying fires:—
Where these are not, I despise
Lovely cheeks or lips or eyes.

T. Carew (1595–1640)

LOVE IS ENOUGH

from Love is Enough

Love is enough: though the World be a-
  waning,
And the woods have no voice but the voice of
  complaining,
  Though the sky be too dark for dim eyes to
    discover
The gold-cups and daisies fair blooming
  thereunder,
Though the hills be held shadows, and the sea
  a dark wonder,
  And this day draw a veil over all deeds
    passed over,
Yet their hands shall not tremble, their feet
  shall not falter;
The void shall not weary, the fear shall not
  alter
  These lips and these eyes of the loved and
    the lover.

William Morris (1834–1896)

A Birthday

My heart is like a singing bird
  Whose nest is in a watered shoot;
My heart is like an apple tree
  Whose boughs are bent with thickset fruit;
My heart is like a rainbow shell
  That paddles in a halcyon sea;
My heart is gladder than all these
  Because my love is come to me.

Raise me a dais of silk and down;
  Hang it with vair and purple dyes;
Carve it in doves and pomegranates
  And peacocks with a hundred eyes;
Work it in gold and silver grapes,
  In leaves and silver fleurs-de-lys;
Because the birthday of my life
  Is come, my love is come to me.

Christina Rossetti (1830–1894)

To Fanny Brawne
8 July 1819

My sweet Girl,
Your letter gave me more delight than anything
in the world but yourself could do; indeed, I am
almost astonished that any absent one should
have the luxurious power over my senses which
I feel. Even when I am not thinking of you,
I perceive your tenderness and a tenderer
nature stealing upon me. All my thoughts, my
unhappiest days and nights, have I find not at all
cured me of my love of Beauty, but made it so
intense that I am miserable that you are not with
me: or rather breathe in that dull sort of patience
that cannot be called Life. I never knew before,
what such a love as you have made me feel, was;
I did not believe in it; my Fancy was afraid of it,
lest it should burn me up. But if you will fully
love me, though there may be some fire, 'twill
not be more than we can bear when moistened
and bedewed with Pleasures. You mention 'hor-
rid people,' and ask me whether it depend upon
them whether I see you again. Do understand
me, my love, in this. I have so much of you in

my heart that I must turn Mentor when I see a chance of harm befalling you. I would never see anything but Pleasure in your eyes, love on your lips, and Happiness in your steps.

John Keats (1795–1821)

from Colossians
Chapter 3, Verses 12–15

As God's chosen ones, holy and beloved, clothe yourselves with compassion, kindness, humility, meekness, and patience. Bear with one another and, if anyone has a complaint against another, forgive each other; just as the Lord has forgiven you, so you also must forgive. Above all, clothe yourselves with love, which binds everything together in perfect harmony. And let the peace of Christ rule in your hearts, to which indeed you were called in the one body. And be thankful.

We Two, How Long We Were Fool'd

We two, how long we were fool'd,

Now transmuted, we swiftly escape as Nature
escapes,

We are Nature, long have we been absent, but
now we return,

We become plants, trunks, foliage, roots, bark,

We are bedded in the ground, we are rocks,

We are oaks, we grow in the openings side by
side,

We browse, we are two among the wild herds
spontaneous as any,

We are two fishes swimming in the sea
together,

We are what locust blossoms are, we drop
scent around lanes mornings and evenings,

We are also the coarse smut of beasts,
vegetables, minerals,

We are two predatory hawks, we soar above
and look down,

We are two resplendent suns, we it is who
balance ourselves orbic and stellar, we are as
two comets,

We prowl fang'd and four-footed in the woods,
  we spring on prey,
We are two clouds forenoons and afternoons
  driving overhead,
We are seas mingling, we are two of those
  cheerful waves rolling over each other and
  interwetting each other,
We are what the atmosphere is, transparent,
  receptive, pervious, impervious,
We are snow, rain, cold, darkness, we are each
  product and influence of the globe,
We have circled and circled till we have
  arrived home again, we two,
We have voided all but freedom and all but
  our own joy.

Walt Whitman (1819–1892)

from Wuthering Heights

He's more myself than I am. Whatever our souls are made of, his and mine are the same [. . .] my great thought in living is himself. If all else perished, and *he* remained, I should still continue to be; and if all else remained, and he were annihilated, the universe would turn to a mighty stranger.

Emily Brontë (1818–1848)

If I Were Loved

If I were loved, as I desire to be,
What is there in the great sphere of the earth,
And range of evil between death and birth,
That I should fear, – if I were loved by thee?
All the inner, all the outer world of pain
Clear love would pierce and cleave, if thou
   wert mine,
As I have heard that, somewhere in the main,
Fresh-water springs come up through bitter
   brine.
'Twere joy, not fear, clasped hand-in-hand
   with thee,
To wait for death – mute – careless of all ills,
Apart upon a mountain, though the surge
Of some new deluge from a thousand hills
Flung leagues of roaring foam into the gorge
Below us, as far on as eye could see.

Alfred, Lord Tennyson (1809–1892)

from Paradise Lost
Book IV

With thee conversing I forget all time,
All seasons and their change, all please alike.
Sweet is the breath of morn, her rising sweet,
With charm of earliest birds; pleasant the sun
When first on this delightful land he spreads
His orient beams, on herb, tree, fruit and
   flower,
Glistering with dew; fragrant the fertile earth
After soft showers; and sweet the coming on
Of grateful evening mild, then silent night
With this her solemn bird and this fair moon,
And these the gems of heaven, her starry train:
But neither breath of morn when she ascends
With charm of earliest birds, nor rising sun
On this delightful land, nor herb, fruit, flower,
Glistering with dew, nor fragrance after showers,
Nor grateful evening mild, nor silent night
With this her solemn bird, nor walk by moon,
Or glittering starlight without thee is sweet.

John Milton (1608–1674)

Night Thoughts

Stars, you are unfortunate, I pity you,
Beautiful as you are, shining in your glory,
Who guide seafaring men through stress and
   peril
And have no recompense from gods or mortals,
Love you do not, nor do you know what love is.
Hours that are aeons urgently conducting
Your figures in a dance through the vast
   heaven,
What journey have you ended in this moment,
Since lingering in the arms of my beloved
I lost all memory of you and midnight.

Johann Wolfgang von Goethe (1749–1832)

Sonnet 116

Let me not to the marriage of true minds
Admit impediments. Love is not love
Which alters when it alteration finds,
Or bends with the remover to remove:
O, no, it is an ever-fixed mark,
That looks on tempests and is never shaken;
It is the star to every wandering bark,
Whose worth's unknown, although his height
  be taken.
Love's not Time's fool, though rosy lips and
  cheeks
Within his bending sickle's compass come;
Love alters not with his brief hours and weeks,
But bears it out even to the edge of doom.
    If this be error and upon me proved,
    I never writ, nor no man ever loved.

William Shakespeare (1564–1616)

First Sight of Her and After

A day is drawing to its fall
  I had not dreamed to see;
The first of many to enthrall
  My spirit, will it be?
Or is this eve the end of all
  Such new delight for me?

I journey home: the pattern grows
  Of moonshades on the way:
'Soon the first quarter, I suppose,'
  Sky-glancing travellers say;
I realize that it, for those,
  Has been a common day.

Thomas Hardy (1840–1928)

When the Heart is Hard

When the heart is hard and parched up, come
upon me with a shower of mercy.

When grace is lost from life, come with a
burst of song.

When tumultuous work raises its din on all
sides shutting me out from beyond, come to
me, my lord of silence, with thy peace and
rest.

When my beggarly heart sits crouched, shut
up in a corner, break open the door, my
king, and come with the ceremony of a king.

When desire blinds the mind with delusion
and dust, O thou holy one, thou wakeful,
come with thy light and thy thunder.

Rabindranath Tagore (1861–1941)

from The Portrait of a Lady

It has made me better loving you [. . .] it has made me wiser, and easier, and brighter. [. . .] I used to want a great many things before and to be angry I didn't have them. Theoretically I was satisfied, I once told you. I flattered myself I had limited my wants. But I was subject to irritation; I used to have morbid, sterile, hateful fits of hunger, of desire. Now I'm really satisfied, because I can't think of anything better. It's just as when one has been trying to spell out a book in the twilight and suddenly the lamp comes in. I had been putting out my eyes over the book of life and finding nothing to reward me for my pains; but now that I can read it properly I see that it's a delightful story.

Henry James (1843–1916)

from Corinthians
Chapter 13 (NRSV)

If I speak in the tongues of mortals and of angels, but do not have love, I am a noisy gong or a clanging cymbal. And if I have prophetic powers, and understand all mysteries and all knowledge, and if I have all faith, so as to remove mountains, but do not have love, I am nothing. If I give away all my possessions, and if I hand over my body so that I may boast, but do not have love, I gain nothing.

Love is patient; love is kind; love is not envious or boastful or arrogant or rude. It does not insist on its own way; it is not irritable or resentful; it does not rejoice in wrongdoing, but rejoices in the truth. It bears all things, believes all things, hopes all things, endures all things.

Love never ends. But as for prophecies, they will come to an end; as for tongues, they will cease; as for knowledge, it will come to an end. For we know only in part, and we prophesy only in part; but when the complete comes, the partial will come to an end. When I was a child, I spoke like a child, I thought like a child, I reasoned like a child; when I became an adult, I put an end to childish ways. For now we see in a mirror, dimly, but then we will see face to face. Now I know only in part; then I will know fully, even as I have been fully known. And now faith, hope, and love abide, these three; and the greatest of these is love.

from 'A Discourse on the Passion of Love'

The more mind we have the greater the passions are, since the passions being only sentiments and thoughts that belong purely to the mind although they are occasioned by the body, it is obvious that they are no longer any thing but the mind itself, and that thus they fill up its entire capacity. I speak here only of the ardent passions, for the others are often mingled together and cause a very annoying confusion; but this is never the case in those who have mind.

In a great soul everything is great.

It is asked whether it is necessary to love? This should not be asked, it should be felt. We do not deliberate upon it, we are forced to it, and take pleasure in deceiving ourselves when we discuss it.

Definiteness of mind causes definiteness of passion; this is why a great and definite mind loves with ardor, and sees distinctly what it loves.

Blaise Pascal, translated by Orlando
Williams Wight
(1623–1662 and 1824–1888)

House of Dreams

You took my empty dreams
  And filled them every one
With tenderness and nobleness,
  April and the sun.

The old empty dreams
  Where my thoughts would throng
Are far too full of happiness
  To even hold a song.

Oh, the empty dreams were dim
  And the empty dreams were wide,
They were sweet and shadowy houses
  Where my thoughts could hide.

But you took my dreams away
  And you made them all come true –
My thoughts have no place now to play,
  And nothing now to do.

Sara Teasdale (1884–1933)

Never Marry But For Love

Never marry but for love;
but see that thou lovest what is lovely.
If love be not the chiefest motive,
thou wilt soon grow weary of a married state
    and stray from thy promise,
to search out thy pleasures in forbidden
    places . . .

Between a man and his wife, nothing ought to
    rule but love . . .
As love ought to bring them together,
so it is the best way to keep them well together.

A husband and wife that love and value one
    another show their children . . .
that they should do so too.
Others visibly lose their authority in their
    families by the contempt of one another,
and teach their children to be unnatural by
    their own example.

Let not enjoyment lessen,
but augment, affection;

it being the basest of passions to like when we
  have not,
what we slight when we possess.

Here it is we ought to search out our pleasure,
where the field is large and full of variety,
and of an enduring nature;
sickness,
poverty or disgrace being not able to shake it
  because it is not under the moving
  influences of worldly contingencies.

Nothing can be more entire and without
  reserve;
nothing more zealous,
affectionate and sincere;
nothing more contented than such a couple,
nor greater temporal felicity than to be one of
  them.

William Penn (1718–1644)

A Moment

The clouds had made a crimson crown
  Above the mountains high.
The stormy sun was going down
  In a stormy sky.

Why did you let your eyes so rest on me,
  And hold your breath between?
In all the ages this can never be
  As if it had not been.

Mary Elizabeth Coleridge (1861–1907)

WEDDED BLISS

Wedded Bliss

'O come and be my mate!' said the Eagle to the
Hen;
        'I love to soar, but then
          I want my mate to rest
          Forever in the nest!'
          Said the Hen, 'I cannot fly,
          I have no wish to try,
But I joy to see my mate careering through the
sky!'
They wed, and cried, 'Ah, this is Love, my
own!'
And the Hen sat, the Eagle soared, alone.

'O come and be my mate!' said the Lion to the
Sheep;
        'My love for you is deep!
          I slay, a Lion should,
          But you are mild and good!'
          Said the sheep, 'I do no ill –
          Could not, had I the will –
But I joy to see my mate pursue, devour and
kill.'

They wed, and cried, 'Ah, this is Love, my
   own!'
And the Sheep browsed, the Lion prowled,
   alone.

'O come and be my mate!' said the Salmon to
   the Clam;
        'You are not wise, but I am,
        I know sea and stream as well,
        You know nothing but your shell.'
        Said the Clam, 'I'm slow of motion,
        But my love is all devotion,
And I joy to have my mate traverse lake and
   stream and ocean!'
They wed, and cried, 'Ah, this is Love, my
   own!'
And the Clam sucked, the Salmon swam, alone.

Charlotte Perkins Gilman (1860–1935)

Love's Garden

A little garden, great enough
　To hold Love's wings.
Yea, and the sacred Bird of Love,
　Hark, how he sings!

The ardent Flower of Love, likewise,
　Burns in the brake.
Love's wings are set with myriad eyes,
　Ever awake.

Heavy with honey flies the bee
　From rose to rose;
Powdered with gold dust to the knee,
　He comes and goes.

The secret song the nightingale
　Sang to the moon,
It shall be hidden by Love's veil,
　Now it is noon.

The secret thing the golden bee
　Said to the rose,

Though it be known to thee and me,
  Shall we disclose?

Ah no! Love's secrets let us keep,
  Lest the winged god,
Angered, go seeking, while we sleep,
  Some new abode.

Katharine Tynan (1861–1931)

from Les Misérables

You can give without loving, but you can never love without giving. The great acts of love are done by those who are habitually performing small acts of kindness. We pardon to the extent that we love. Love is knowing that even when you are alone, you will never be lonely again. And great happiness of life is the conviction that we are loved. Loved for ourselves. And even loved in spite of ourselves.

Victor Hugo (1802–1885)

Wild Nights

Wild nights! Wild nights!
Were I with thee,
Wild nights should be
Our luxury!

Futile the winds
To a heart in port, –
Done with the compass,
Done with the chart.

Rowing in Eden!
Ah! the sea!
Might I but moor
To-night in thee!

Emily Dickinson (1830–1886)

O Solitude! if I must with thee dwell

O Solitude! if I must with thee dwell,
Let it not be among the jumbled heap
Of murky buildings; climb with me the steep,—
Nature's observatory—whence the dell,
Its flowery slopes, its river's crystal swell,
May seem a span; let me thy vigils keep
'Mongst boughs pavillion'd, where the deer's
    swift leap
Startles the wild bee from the fox-glove bell.
But though I'll gladly trace these scenes with
    thee,
Yet the sweet converse of an innocent mind,
Whose words are images of thoughts refin'd,
Is my soul's pleasure; and it sure must be
Almost the highest bliss of human-kind,
When to thy haunts two kindred spirits flee.

John Keats (1795–1821)

from My Ántonia

I was something that lay under the sun and felt
it, like the pumpkins, and I did not want to be
anything more. I was entirely happy. Perhaps we
feel like that when we die and become a part of
something entire, whether it is sun and air, or
goodness and knowledge. At any rate, that is
happiness; to be dissolved into something com-
plete and great. When it comes to one, it comes
as naturally as sleep.

Willa Cather (1873–1947)

from Song of Solomon
Chapter 2, Verses 8-12

The voice of my beloved!
  Look, he comes,
leaping upon the mountains,
  bounding over the hills.
My beloved is like a gazelle
  or a young stag.
Look, there he stands
  behind our wall,
gazing in at the windows,
  looking through the lattice.
My beloved speaks and says to me:
'Arise, my love, my fair one,
  and come away;
for now the winter is past,
  the rain is over and gone.
The flowers appear on the earth;
  the time of singing has come,
and the voice of the turtle-dove
  is heard in our land.

from To Althea, From Prison

Stone Walls do not a Prison make,
Nor Iron bars a Cage;
Minds innocent and quiet take
That for an Hermitage.
If I have freedom in my Love,
And in my soul am free,
Angels alone that soar above,
Enjoy such Liberty.

Richard Lovelace (1617–1657)

Song

Two doves upon the selfsame branch,
   Two lilies on a single stem,
Two butterflies upon one flower: –
   Oh happy they who look on them!

Who look upon them hand in hand
   Flushed in the rosy summer light;
Who look upon them hand in hand,
   And never give a thought to night.

Christina Rossetti (1830–1894)

The Owl and the Pussy-Cat

The Owl and the Pussy-Cat went to sea
  In a beautiful pea-green boat.
They took some honey, and plenty of money
  Wrapped up in a five-pound note.
The Owl looked up to the stars above,
  And sang to a small guitar,
'O lovely Pussy! O Pussy, my love,
What a beautiful Pussy you are,
        You are,
        You are!
What a beautiful Pussy you are!'

Pussy said to the Owl, 'You elegant fowl!
  How charmingly sweet you sing!
O let us be married! too long we have tarried:
  But what shall we do for a ring?'
They sailed away, for a year and a day,
  To the land where the Bong-Tree grows,
And there in a wood a Piggy-wig stood,
With a ring at the end of his nose,
        His nose,
        His nose!
With a ring at the end of his nose.

'Dear Pig, are you willing to sell for one
   shilling
      Your ring?' Said the Piggy, 'I will.'
So they took it away, and were married next
   day
      By the turkey who lives on the hill.
They dined on mince, and slices of quince,
      Which they ate with a runcible spoon;

And hand in hand, on the edge of the sand
They danced by the light of the moon,
               The moon,
               The moon,
They danced by the light of the moon.

Edward Lear (1812–1888)

from The Secret Garden

One of the strange things about living in the world is that it is only now and then one is quite sure one is going to live forever and ever and ever. One knows it sometimes when one gets up at the tender solemn dawn-time and goes out and stands alone and throws one's head far back and looks up and up and watches the pale sky slowly changing and flushing and marvelous unknown things happening until the East almost makes one cry out and one's heart stands still at the strange unchanging majesty of the rising of the sun – which has been happening every morning for thousands and thousands and thousands of years. One knows it then for a moment or so. And one knows it sometimes when one stands by oneself in a wood at sunset and the mysterious deep gold stillness slanting through and under the branches seems to be saying slowly again and again something one cannot quite hear, however much one tries. Then sometimes the immense quiet of the dark blue at night with millions of stars waiting and watching makes one sure; and sometimes a

sound of far-off music makes it true; and some-
times a look in someone's eyes.

Frances Hodgson Burnett (1849–1924)

Friendship

Oh, the comfort –
the inexpressible comfort of feeling *safe* with
  a person –
having neither to weigh thoughts nor measure
  words,
but pouring them all right out,
just as they are,
chaff and grain together;
certain that a faithful hand will take and sift
  them,
keep what is worth keeping,
and then with the breath of kindness blow the
  rest away.

Dinah Maria Craik (1826–1887)

Camomile Tea

Outside the sky is light with stars;
There's a hollow roaring from the sea.
And, alas! for the little almond flowers,
The wind is shaking the almond tree.

How little I thought, a year ago,
In the horrible cottage upon the Lee,
That he and I should be sitting so
And sipping a cup of camomile tea.

Light as feathers the witches fly,
The horn of the moon is plain to see;
By a firefly under a jonquil flower
A goblin toasts a bumble-bee.

We might be fifty, we might be five,
So snug, so compact, so wise are we!
Under the kitchen-table leg
My knee is pressing against his knee.

Katherine Mansfield (1888–1923)

Love Song

When my soul touches yours a great chord
    sings!
How shall I tune it then to other things?
O! That some spot in darkness could be found
That does not vibrate whene'er your depth
    sound.
But everything that touches you and me
Welds us as played strings sound one melody.
Where is the instrument whence the sounds
    flow?
And whose the master-hand that holds the
    bow?
O! Sweet song—

Rainer Maria Rilke (1875–1926),
translated by Jessie Lamont

from Emma

The wedding was very much like other weddings, where the parties have no taste for finery or parade; and Mrs. Elton, from the particulars detailed by her husband, thought it all extremely shabby, and very inferior to her own. 'Very little white satin, very few lace veils; a most pitiful business! Selina would stare when she heard of it.'—But, in spite of these deficiencies, the wishes, the hopes, the confidence, the predictions of the small band of true friends who witnessed the ceremony, were fully answered in the perfect happiness of the union.

Jane Austen (1775–1817)

A Spring Morning

The Spring comes in with all her hues and
    smells,
In freshness breathing over hills and dells;
O'er woods where May her gorgeous drapery
    flings,
And meads washed fragrant by their laughing
    springs.
Fresh are new opened flowers, untouched and
    free
From the bold rifling of the amorous bee.
The happy time of singing birds is come,
And Love's lone pilgrimage now finds a home;
Among the mossy oaks now coos the dove,
And the hoarse crow finds softer notes for
    love.
The foxes play around their dens, and bark
In joy's excess, 'mid woodland shadows dark.
The flowers join lips below; the leaves above;
And every sound that meets the ear is Love.

John Clare (1793–1864)

from 'The Bells'

Hear the mellow wedding bells,
     Golden bells!
What a world of happiness their harmony
   foretells!
    Through the balmy air of night
    How they ring out their delight!
     From the molten-golden notes,
       And all in tune,
     What a liquid ditty floats
To the turtle-dove that listens, while she
   gloats
      On the moon!
    Oh, from out the sounding cells,
What a gush of euphony voluminously wells!
     How it swells!
     How it dwells
    On the Future! how it tells
    Of the rapture that impels
   To the swinging and the ringing
    Of the bells, bells, bells,
   Of the bells, bells, bells, bells,

Bells, bells, bells—
To the rhyming and the chiming of the bells!

Edgar Allan Poe (1809–1849)

from Chamber Music
Poem VI

I would in that sweet bosom be
    (O sweet it is and fair it is!)
Where no rude wind might visit me.
    Because of sad austerities
I would in that sweet bosom be.

I would be ever in that heart
    (O soft I knock and soft entreat her!)
Where only peace might be my part.
    Austerities were all the sweeter
So I were ever in that heart.

James Joyce (1882–1941)

To-night

The moon is a curving flower of gold,
  The sky is still and blue;
The moon was made for the sky to hold,
  And I for you.

The moon is a flower without a stem,
  The sky is luminous;
Eternity was made for them,
  To-night for us.

Sara Teasdale (1884–1933)

Public Speaking Tips

Warm Up:

If you've time before the reading; close your eyes, breathe deeply in through the nose and out through the mouth.

Visualize each breath coming up from the ground and rising through your body, filling the body with energy, confidence and stability. Repeat this five times.

Body-language Basics:

Take *hands out of pockets* (hands in pockets can make you look less engaged or nervous).

Eye contact – make sure you look up and out when you're speaking. When you practice, place cushions around the room and direct one line of your reading to each.

Voice Essentials:

The pace of your reading should be conversational.

Volume – try singing your reading when no one's around. It's a brilliant way to empower your voice.

Pause – don't be afraid to use it! Pausing can add emphasis and create suspense, and it can allow the audience to process what you've said.

Energy – be intentional about the energy you bring to the reading; if you have energy, your audience will be engaged.

Smile! – try saying 'I feel very happy' with a sad face; you will notice how this affects the tone of your voice. Smiling will make your voice more musical and will relax your audience.

Index of Poets and Authors

Austen, Jane   153

Bradstreet, Anne   92
Brontë, Charlotte   51
Brontë, Emily   72, 116
Browning, Elizabeth Barrett   5, 88
Browning, Robert   12, 16, 26
Bulwer-Lytton, Edward Robert   60
Burnett, Frances Hodgson   148
Burns, Robert   61
Byron, Lord   18

Carew, T.   105
Cather, Willa   142
Clare, John   10, 154
Coleridge, Mary Elizabeth   131
Coleridge, Samuel Taylor   8
Craik, Dinah Maria   150
Cummings, E. E.   45

de Bernières, Louis   97
Dickens, Charles   104
Dickinson, Emily   140
Donne, John   43, 64

Eliot, George   76

Fitzgerald, F. Scott   20
Fletcher, John   41

Gibran, Kahlil   87
Gilman, Charlotte Perkins   135

Hardy, Thomas   121
Heaney, Seamus   102
Hugo, Victor   139

James, Clive   58
James, Henry   123
Johnson, James Weldon   54
Joyce, James   157

Keats, John   75, 96, 111, 141

Landon, Letitia Elizabeth   55
Lawrence, D. H.   89
Lear, Edward   146
Lindbergh, Anne Morrow   73
Lovelace, Richard   144
Lowell, Amy   35

Mansfield, Katherine   39, 151
Mew, Charlotte   24
Meynell, Alice   30
Millay, Edna St. Vincent   103
Milton, John   118
Monroe, Harriet   47
Moore, Thomas   36
Morris, William   109
Murdoch, Iris   34

Pascal, Blaise   126
Peele, George   29
Penn, William   129
Peterson, Wilferd A.   93
Philips, Katherine   62
Plato   27
Poe, Edgar Allan   155

Raleigh, Sir Walter   6
Rilke, Rainer Maria   152
Rossetti, Christina   83, 110, 145
Rumi   13

Scott, Sir Walter   77
Shakespeare, William   4, 82, 120
Shelley, Percy Bysshe   3
Sidney, Sir Philip   17
Stevenson, Robert Louis   9, 40
Suckling, Sir John   14
Sylvester, J.   95

Tagore, Rabindranath   122
Teasdale, Sara   128, 158
Tennyson, Alfred, Lord   57, 85, 117
Tessimond, A. S. J   22
Thoreau, Henry David   79
Twain, Mark   33, 70
Tynan, Katharine   137

Verhaeren, Emile   98
von Goethe, Johann Wolfgang   119

Wells, Jane   53
Wharton, Edith   21
Whitman, Walt   49, 114

Yeats, W. B., 52, 69

Index of First Lines

A day is drawing to its fall   121
A good marriage must be created   93
A little garden, great enough   137
A thing of beauty is a joy for ever   96
An hour with thee! When earliest day   77
And when one of them meets with his other half   27
As God's chosen ones, holy and beloved   113

Bright Star! would I were steadfast as thou art   75

Come live with me, and be my love   43
Come, let me take thee to my breast   61

Do you ask what the birds say? The Sparrow,
    the Dove   8

Fidelity and love are two different things, like a
    flower and a gem   89
From our low seat beside the fire   24

Had I the heavens' embroidered cloths   52
Have you got a biro I can borrow?   58
He smiled understandingly – much more than
    understandingly   20
He that loves a rosy cheek   105
He's more myself than I am   116
Hear the mellow wedding bells   155

How do I love thee? Let me
  count the ways 5

I ask but one thing of you, only one 35
I cannot promise you a life of sunshine 33
i carry your heart with me 45
I did not live until this time 62
I have for the first time found what I can
  truly love 51
I hereby give myself. I love you 34
I love my life, but not too well 47
I loved you first; but afterwards your love 83
I must not think of thee; and, tired yet strong 30
I ne'er was struck before that hour 10
I prithee send me back my heart 14
I suppose there is one friend in the life of
  each of us 21
I think awhile of Love, and while I think 79
I was something that lay under the sun and
  felt it 142
I will make you brooches and toys for your
  delight 40
I wonder by my troth, what thou and I 64
I would in that sweet bosom be 157
If ever two were one, then surely we 92
If I speak in the tongues of mortals and of
  angels 124
If I were loved, as I desire to be 117
If thou must love me, let it be for nought 88
It has made me better loving you 123

Let me not to the marriage of true minds 120
Let your love be stronger than your hate or
    anger 53
Light, so low upon earth 85
Listen! I will be honest with you 49
Livy darling 70
Love had no other desire but to fulfil itself 87
Love is a temporary madness 97
Love is enough: though the World be
    a-waning 109
Love is like the wild rose briar 72
Love should run out to meet love with open arms 9
Love thee! yes, yes! the storms that rend aside 55

Masons, when they start upon a building 102
My darling 39
My heart is like a singing bird 110
My sweet Girl 111
My true-love hath my heart, and I have his 17

Never marry but for love 129
No sooner met, but they look'd, no sooner 4
Now sleeps the crimson petal, now the white 57
Now what is love, I pray thee tell? 6
Now you will feel no rain 42

'O come and be my mate!' said the Eagle to the
    Hen 135
O divine star of Heaven 41
O Solitude! if I must with thee dwell 141
O talk not to me of a name great in story 18

Oh, the comfort 150

One of the strange things about living in the
    world 148

Out of your whole life give but a moment! 26

Outside the sky is light with stars 151

Set me as a seal upon your heart 38

Shall I compare thee to a summer's day? 82

Since we parted yester eve 60

Stars, you are unfortunate, I pity you 119

Step by step, day by day 98

Stone Walls do not a Prison make 144

The clouds had made a crimson crown 131

The dawning of morn, the daylight's
    sinking 36

The fountains mingle with the river 3

The grey sea and the long black land 12

The minute I heard my first love story 13

The moon is a curving flower of gold 158

The more mind we have the greater the
    passions 126

The Owl and the Pussy-Cat went to sea 146

The Spring comes in with all her hues
    and smells 154

The voice of my beloved 143

The wedding was very much like other
    weddings 153

Two doves upon the selfsame branch 145

We two, how long we were fool'd 114

Were I as base as is the lowly plain 95
What greater thing is there for two human souls 76
What thing is love? for, well I wot, love is a thing 29
When buffeted and beaten by life's storms 54
When I first met you I knew I had come
    at last home 22
When my soul touches yours a great chord
    sings 152
When the heart is hard and parched up, come
    upon me with a shower of mercy 122
When two people are at one in their inmost
    hearts 84
When we are old and these rejoicing veins 103
When you are old and grey and full of sleep 69
When you love someone you do not love them all
    the time 73
Wild nights! Wild nights! 140
With thee conversing I forget all time 118

You are part of my existence, part of myself 104
You can give without loving, but you can never love
    without giving 139
You took my empty dreams 128
You will only expect a few words 16

Permission acknowledgements